I0599697

William
And The
Seventh Silence

TIGRESS

i

Published by:
Tigress Sounds & Publishing Inc.
New York, USA
First Edition: July 2025

For more information about our books, visit:
www.TigressPublishing.com

Cover Design by Tigress

Printed in the United States of America.

TABLE OF CONTENTS

DEDICATION

For my son, my light in the quiet.

You didn't just inspire William.

You are the stillness behind his strength,

The Echo behind his courage,

The reason the silence always had meaning.

In your questions, I found plot.

In your brilliance, I found magic.

And in your presence, I found the boy who could hold the world's truth.

And still laugh at cafeteria meat cubes.

This story is your inheritance —

crafted from our shared dreams,

carried on the back of your imagination,

And sealed with love deeper than ink.

May you always hear the things others miss,

And remember that you were never meant to be quiet.

    With all my love,

    Mom.

Dramatis Lexicon

Your Guide Through the Intricacies of This Book.

1. The Archive:

A vast, invisible realm where truth is kept, guarded, and sometimes hidden. It is a living, breathing memory system, not neutral, not fixed. It can be rewritten, corrupted, or weaponized. It appears as a shifting classroom (Room 207C) but exists across dimensions.

"The Archive is not a library. It's a weapon."

2. The Silences (First–Seventh Silence):

Each Silence represents a foundational truth buried before language. Not what was said, but what remained unspoken, was erased or feared. The Seventh Silence is the most dangerous. It was never meant to be spoken. When broken, it causes memory itself to unravel. Each Silence is tied to truths that could destabilize power if revealed.

3. The Codex

An ancient, living entity that records forgotten or censored truths; truths the Archive won't store. It responds to touch and can trigger prophetic visions. Prophecies it reveals cannot be fully trusted, as even prophecy can be rewritten.

"The Codex is a lie detector. It remembers what the Archive tries to forget."

4. Keepers/Nyimi

Chosen from ancient bloodlines, Keepers are those born to hear and preserve truths that were never written down. William is a descendant of Keepers, unknowingly carrying the resonance of the

First Silence. Keepers are part-guardian, part-truth-teller, often marked by their ability to hear what others can't.

"You were never meant to find the Archive. You were meant to be it."

5. Curators

The high stewards of the Archive — part historian, part enforcer. Curators decide which truths are preserved, which are rewritten, and which are erased entirely. They are the Archive's voice, its memory-keepers, and its quiet gatekeepers of forgetting. While they claim to protect history, they often shape it.

6. The Heretic

A former Keeper who refused the Archive's rules and sought to reveal the Seventh Silence. Viewed as a traitor by the Curators, but seen by the Echoes as a revolutionary. His legacy haunts the story, suggesting that even truth keepers can become threats.

7. The Echoes

A hidden group that opposes the Archive's censorship. They preserve what was erased, what never made it into memory, and truths that challenge official narratives. Their motto: "Speak what they erased."

8. The Rewrite

A mysterious force, possibly conscious, that is editing history in real time. It erases names, removes photos, and distorts family trees. Its arrival marks the collapse of memory's reliability. William is revealed to be the one original memory the Rewrite cannot alter.

9. The Unwritten Word

A mythic symbol/language predating all others, so powerful it was never meant to be spoken or drawn. Lilith, William's sister, begins to draw them.

Prologue

The First Silence

Circa 3000 BCE—Valley of the White Nile, Nubian Highlands

The boy was no older than twelve when they crowned him Keeper, but his eyes held the weight of a man who had already lived a thousand years.

His true name was lost in the tongues of time, traded for symbols carved in stone and breath. But in the sacred hills where the wind did not whistle but listened, he was called Ashem, *He Who Hears the Unheard.*

The elders came barefoot, cloaked in Kente and white ash, circling him beneath a moon that hung swollen and full, seemingly too heavy for the sky. Around them, the flames of seven clay lanterns flickered, each one holding the memory of a Silence. The air tasted of clay smoke, sweet river reed, and the metallic tang of ozone. Ash cooled on bare feet; the White Nile murmured like a low, steady drumbeat against the earth.

But only one lantern had never been lit.

"This," said Elder Chuma, his voice rough with age as he placed a sealed scroll in the boy's trembling hands, "is the truth the world will not be ready for. Not today. Not in this life. Nor in the next."

"Why hide it?" Ashem asked. He tried to keep his voice steady, but the scroll felt heavy, denser than wood or parchment should be.

"Because truth burns louder than lies when lit too early," Chuma whispered, leaning close. "And the world, my son, is soaked in dry grass."

The scroll was wrapped in bark made from trees that no longer grew, bound in string woven from lion's mane and storm hair. Upon its surface was no ink, just a single ripple, like the soft imprint of breath on glass.

"You must take it to the Vault," Chuma said. "And you must not speak of it again. Not until the Silence calls itself home."

The boy nodded. He understood. It was not a burden of carrying; it was a burden of keeping.

And so began his descent into the Temple of the Unwritten, where no name was ever spoken and sound itself bowed before stone.

He walked alone for forty nights through corridors of absolute stillness, past the bones of languages forgotten, and past visions that whispered not in words, but in knowing. The darkness here was not empty; it was full. He entered the chamber of the Seventh Silence.

And there, with bare feet and bloodied fingers, he carved the final sigil, one no living tongue could pronounce, onto a slab of black stone.

Then he placed the scroll into the Vault. As the stone lid slid shut, the ground didn't shake. It hummed. It was a soundless quake, a vibration that rattled the teeth but made no noise.

The world above shifted. The truth was hidden.

The boy was never seen again. But his gift? That would echo down bloodlines, across centuries, jumping like a spark through time, until it landed in a city far from these sands.

Into a boy who would hear too much. A boy who would listen when the world stopped.

A boy called William.

CHAPTER

1

Whispers in the Lunchroom

William Vale was trying very hard not to explode.

Not because of some world-ending catastrophe, at least, not yet, but because the sensory assault of the seventh-grade cafeteria was currently registering at an eleven on his internal Richter scale.

The air smelled of industrial disinfectant, wet sneakers, and something that was legally required to be labeled "pizza." The noise was a physical thing, a wall of shrieks, slamming trays, and the rhythmic thumping of a hip-hop track leaking from someone's speaker. It battered against William's skull, finding every crack.

And then there was Jesse Tran.

Jesse, his best friend and a human disaster in motion, sat across from him, grinning like a shark who had just discovered an all-you-can-eat buffet. He had just dared William to eat three cafeteria "meat cubes" stacked on top of each other like a flesh-Jenga tower.

"They jiggle like they know what they've done," Jesse whispered, leaning in with an expression that resembled horror mixed with admiration.

William poked the cubes with a plastic fork. They didn't just jiggle. They trembled. The fork tine bent slightly, as if the meat were fighting back.

"You're stalling," Jesse said, tapping his fingers on the table. "Eat it or admit defeat. The Council of Cubes demands a sacrifice."

"I'd rather lick a chalkboard. In fact, I'd rather lick Mr. Drexler's chalkboard."

"Bold words from a coward."

William sighed, the sound lost in the cacophony of the room. "Fine."

He stabbed the cube tower and popped the monstrosity into his mouth, instantly regretting every life decision that led to this moment. The texture was wrong; rubbery yet sandy? It tasted like burned tire, and possibly... mint toothpaste?

He swallowed, made a face like he'd just been hexed, and chugged half his water bottle.

"Ladies and gentlemen," Jesse announced to the table, gesturing like a magician revealing a tiger, "I give you William the Indigestible!"

William rolled his eyes, trying not to laugh. This was what made Jesse bearable, even when he was completely unbearable. Jesse was loud, yes, but he was happy loud. He turned everything into a game, a dare, or a reason to laugh. He was the anchor that kept William from drifting away into the noise.

Which was why William hadn't told him about the whispers.

It had started two weeks ago. At first, he thought it was just tinnitus, the wind, the radiator hissing, or the teacher's voice echoing in the hallway. But then it started happening in places where silence was the only sound.

In his bedroom at night, staring at the ceiling fan.

In the library, where even pages turned like they were afraid to interrupt.

And the voices didn't speak like people. They didn't have accents or pitch. They spoke like ideas inserted directly into his brain stem.

Truth left untold is still alive.

Some lies echo louder in silence.

Find the one who writes without ink...

He hadn't told his parents. His older brother, Darius, would laugh and tell him to stop playing video games. His little sister, Lilith, would probably stare at him with those uncomfortably knowing eyes and say something deeply unsettling, like, "I hear them, too. One of them said, 'You're late.'"

Nope. Better to keep it locked inside.

Suddenly, a sharp ringing sound pierced his right ear—high-pitched and violent. William flinched, dropping his fork. He clamped a hand over his ear.

"Whoa," Jesse said, his smile dropping. "You okay? You got that 'I'm-listening-to-ghosts-again' face."

"What does that even mean?" William gritted out, the ringing slowly fading into a dull throb.

"Means you're doing that zone-out thing where you look like you're solving a murder in your head. Seriously, Will, you look pale."

William hesitated. The cafeteria noise surged back in—trays clattering and laughter screaming. He looked at Jesse, the one person who hadn't rewritten him yet.

"If someone told you they could... hear things no one else could, like, actual voices, what would you say?"

Jesse raised a brow, picking up a tater tot. "Are we talking voices-voices? Or, like, an internal monologue with guest stars? Because if it's guest stars, I hope it's Zendaya."

William slumped. "Just forget it."

"Too late. I've decided you're either haunted or chosen. Either way, I'm in. I've always wanted to be the comedic sidekick in a supernatural drama. I have great scream dynamics."

William managed a weak smile. Jesse was ridiculous but loyal.

The bell rang, shattering the conversation. The stampede began—lockers slammed, sneakers squeaked, and somebody down the hall yelled, "YOLO," like it was still 2011.

William walked beside Jesse toward their next class: history with Mr. Drexler, a man who blinked too much and probably hated children. But as William reached for his locker, his hand stopped inches from the metal.

The air around the combination dial wasn't just cold. It was ancient. It radiated a chill that had nothing to do with the school's AC and everything to do with a sealed tomb.

He spun the dial.

Click.

Click.

Click.

He swung the door open.

The smell hit him first, not the usual gym sock bouquet, but a sharp, metallic tang of ozone and sweet river clay. Inside, perfectly folded on top of his math textbook, lay a piece of parchment that defied the laws of the timeline. Its edges were browned with age, the fiber coarse and woven.

It was written in symbols William didn't recognize, jagged geometry that hurt his eyes, yet his brain translated them before he could look away.

At the bottom, in letters that looked like they'd been pressed with silence itself, were four words that made the noise of the hallway vanish completely:

"The Seventh Is Breaking."

CHAPTER 2

The Substitute with No Past

William stared at the note for so long that he forgot how to breathe.

The Seventh Is Breaking.

The letters vibrated, meaning more than mere words, not just in his eyes, but in his chest, like they'd always been there… waiting. The symbols above it wasn't random either. They shimmered slightly, shifting as if they weren't written but alive.

"Earth to William," Jesse said, poking his temple. "What's that? Old homework from another dimension?"

"It was in my locker."

"…Okay, but you didn't put it there?"

"Nope."

"Then clearly we're dealing with one of three possibilities: one, a rogue history teacher from the 1300s, two, a ghost mail, or three, a time-traveling me from the future trying to mess with your head."

William didn't laugh this time.

"Okay," Jesse said slowly, "so we're actually creeped out?" William nodded.

Jesse leaned closer to inspect the note, then instantly recoiled. "Nope. That's ancient. That's cursed. That's some Tomb of the Forgotten Librarian nonsense. I'm out."

But William didn't move. Because beneath the swirl of panic and confusion... Something strange was happening. He wasn't afraid.

He felt... awake.

History class was eerily quiet. Mr. Drexler wasn't there. Instead, there was a substitute standing at the front of the room. She wore all black, not in the dramatic goth way, but in the I've-just-walked-out-of-another-century way.

Her white hair was coiled into a bun so tight it looked carved from stone. Her cane leaned beside her like a relic, and when she turned toward the class, her left eye flashed, not with light, but with something behind it. Something watching.

"Good morning," she said. Her voice was soft, but it landed like thunder. "I am Professor Morrin. Mr. Drexler has... stepped away."

"Forever?" Jesse whispered. William elbowed him.

"Open your books to page one hundred forty-two," Morrin said, "or don't. The truth is not in the book."

The class looked at each other. No one moved.

"William Vale," she said suddenly. He jolted.

"Would you mind standing?"

Jesse grinned. "Ooooh, you're famous now."

William stood slowly, heart thudding.

"What do you know of the Kushite Archives?" Morrin asked. The room froze.

"The... what?" She smiled, barely.

"Never mind. Sit down."

He did. His palms were sweating. He could feel her gaze still burning into him.

Morrin turned back to the board and began writing in symbols William had just seen, the same ones from the note. Identical.

"There were once seven silences," she said, "each born before language. One of them was stolen. One of them was shattered. And one of them… was never meant to be spoken again."

CHAPTER
3

The Room That Wasn't There Yesterday

The bell rang, a shrill, jarring sound that shattered the heavy stillness like glass dropped on tile.

The spell broke. Chairs scraped, zippers hissed, and the stampede for the door began. The students moved with the desperate urgency of inmates released from a holding cell, eager to escape the ozone-scented air.

"Mr. Vale," Morrin's voice cut through the cacophony, not loud, but impossible to ignore. "Perhaps you'll stay a moment."

Jesse, who had been halfway out of his seat, paused. He looked between William and the woman standing like a monolith at the front of the room.

"I'll wait by the door," Jesse whispered, leaning in. "If I hear screaming, I'm calling the Avengers."

"Just go," William muttered, though his throat felt tight.

"Seriously. Screaming. Avengers." Jesse shot one last suspicious look at the substitute and vanished into the hallway.

As the room emptied, the air grew heavy again. William remained standing, his hands gripping the back of his chair. He looked at the blackboard, expecting to see the static chalk lines of the jagged symbol.

Instead, the dust was moving.

It wasn't fading; it was rearranging itself. The white particles drifted across the slate like iron filings pulled by a magnet, swirling until they formed a single, elegant word:

Welcome.

William blinked, and just as quickly as it had formed, the word dissolved into innocent clouds of white dust.

Professor Morrin hadn't moved. She stood with one hand resting on the silver head of her driftwood cane, the other hovering over a notebook that looked less like paper and more like pressed bark.

"Come closer, William," she said.

He forced his legs to move. The distance from his desk to the front of the room felt like miles. When he stopped in front of her, the smell of ozone was stronger, mixed now with something else. Old paper? No. Parchment.

"You saw it," she said. It wasn't a question.

"The word on the board?"

"The shift." She tapped the notebook. "Most minds reject the rearrangement of matter. They see only what they expect to see. You saw the dust move."

William hesitated. "I... I think I need to go to the nurse."

"You don't need a nurse, Mr. Vale. You need a guide."

She opened the notebook. The pages were blank, but as William watched, ink began to bleed onto the surface, not from a pen, but rising from the paper itself.

"The Seventh Silence is not a metaphor," Morrin said, her mismatched eyes boring into his. "It is a lock. And someone has just picked it."

"Who?" William asked, the word escaping before he could check it.

"The enemy of stillness," she replied, though the answer explained nothing. With a quick, violent motion, she tore the page from the notebook. The sound wasn't like paper ripping; it sounded like fabric being sheared.

She held the page out to him. "Room 207C. Third floor. End of the east wing. Do not be late."

William took the paper. The ink was still wet, warm against his thumb. "What happens if I don't go?"

Morrin leaned forward, the gold in her right eye catching the fluorescent light. "Then you will remain deaf to the noise that is coming. And the noise, Mr. Vale, destroys everything it touches."

She turned her back on him, dismissing him as effectively as if she'd pushed him out the door.

William stumbled backward, turned, and fled.

***

The hallway was an assault of normalcy. Lockers slammed. Someone shouted about a lost gym shoe. The air smelled of cheap body spray and stale sandwiches. The ozone was gone.

Jesse was leaning against a row of lockers, scrolling on his phone. When he saw William, he straightened up, scanning him for injuries.

"Okay, you're alive," Jesse said. "Did she give you a detention? Or did she just try to recruit you for a cult?"

William looked down at the paper in his hand. He expected to see the bleeding ink, the jagged symbols, the warning about the lock.

But the ink had settled. The parchment texture was gone, replaced by standard-issue pink slip paper.

DETENTION SLIP

Student: William Vale

Infraction: Disruptive Curiosity

Location: Room 207C

"Just detention," William lied, his voice sounding hollow to his own ears. He held up the slip so Jesse could see.

Jesse squinted at it. "Disruptive curiosity? That's a new one. And where the heck is Room 207C?"

William frowned. "What do you mean?"

"Dude," Jesse laughed, shaking his head. "The east wing ends at Room 205. There is no 207."

Jesse paused, a french fry halfway to his mouth. "Maybe, maybe...that's a myth. Or a typo."

"She said it's there today."

"Right. And I'm the King of England." Jesse dropped the fry. "Look, I like an adventure, but this feels... heavy. Do you want me to come? Safety in numbers? Human shield?"

William looked at his friend, the way Jesse tried to make a joke out of the fear in his eyes. "No," William said. "I think... I think I have to do this alone. It feels private. Like a secret I haven't been told yet."

"Okay," Jesse said, visibly relieved but trying to hide it. "Just... text me if you find a portal. Or if you die. Actually, don't text me if you die. That would be traumatic."

When the final bell rang, the sound vibrated in William's teeth.

He waited until the hallways cleared, until the janitors began their rhythmic sweeping, before he moved. He walked past the library, smelling of floor wax and old paper. He walked past the math wing, smelling of graphite and anxiety.

He climbed the stairs to the second floor.

He walked to the end of the hall, past Room 205.

Past the janitor's closet.

And there, where the mural of the school mascot, a slightly deranged-looking hawk, should have been, was a door.

It shouldn't have been there. The geometry of the hallway didn't allow for it. It was squeezed into a space that hadn't existed ten seconds ago.

The door was heavy, made of dark, ancient wood that seemed to absorb the hallway light. It was etched with symbols that looked burned into the grain, patterns that hurt his eyes if he stared too long. There was no doorknob. Just a circular indentation in the center, the size of a palm.

William's heart hammered a frantic rhythm against his ribs. Run, a part of him whispered. Go home. Play video games. Forget the eye-lady.

But his hand reached out on its own.

As his skin touched the wood, the door let out a sound, not a creak, but a sigh. A click echoed from deep inside the wood, like a heavy lock tumbling open, and the door swung inward.

The air that rushed out wasn't stale classroom air. It was cold, crisp, and smelled of things that didn't belong in a school: burning beeswax, old leather, and the metallic tang of a storm.

William stepped over the threshold.

The door clicked shut behind him.

He wasn't in a classroom.

The ceiling was gone, or at least, it was too high to see, lost in shadows that seemed to breathe. Shelves spiraled upward, defying gravity, packed with scrolls, glass jars filled with shifting smoke, and feathers that glowed with their own light.

A map was suspended mid-air in the center of the room, not hanging, floating. It was made of golden light, displaying continents that had shifted millions of years ago, or perhaps hadn't formed yet.

And standing beside a circular table made of obsidian was Professor Morrin.

"Welcome to the Archive," she said.

William spun in a slow circle, his sneakers squeaking on a floor made of polished stone. "This is... this is impossible."

"This is necessary," she corrected. "It has been waiting for you, William."

"Me? Why me? I'm just... I'm nobody. I get C's in Spanish."

"Language is more than grammar," she said, stepping closer. The obsidian table pulsed with a faint, rhythmic light, like a heartbeat. "You are descended from a lineage of Listeners. The Nyimi. The Keepers."

"The what?"

"Guardians of memory. Preservers of the truth that history tries to pave over." She reached into the pocket of her robe and pulled out a small, wooden ring. It was rough-hewn, simple, but etched with the same spiral symbol.

"This belonged to your great-grandmother," she said softly. "She was the last to hear the Archive sing."

William took the ring. It was warm, vibrating against his skin like a purring cat. "What happened to her?"

Morrin's expression tightened. For a second, the storm in her left eye darkened. "She disappeared. After the Sixth Silence broke."

"So... what's the Seventh?"

The room seemed to dim. The floating map flickered.

"The one," Morrin whispered, "that was never supposed to be awakened."

***

That night, the silence in William's bedroom felt different. It wasn't empty; it was watching.

He sat at his desk, the wooden ring sitting in a pool of lamplight. He had opened his journal to write it all down, the door, the map, the woman, but the pen hovered over the paper. The words wouldn't come. They felt too small.

The door creaked.

William jumped, spinning around.

Lilith stood there. She was six, wearing pajamas covered in cartoon stars, her hair a riot of curls. But she wasn't looking at him. She was looking at the ring.

"Will?" she said. Her voice was small, but steady.

"Hey, munchkin," William breathed, his heart slowing down. "You scared me. What's up?"

She stepped into the room, her bare feet silent on the carpet. "You shouldn't write it down."

William froze. "What?"

She looked up at him, her eyes wide and impossibly dark. "The Archive doesn't like to be seen, Will. It likes to be heard."

A chill walked down William's spine, icy and sharp. "Lilith... how do you know that word?"

She tilted her head, as if listening to a sound he couldn't hear. "She told me you'd ask that."

"Who?"

Lilith smiled. It wasn't her usual gummy, missing-tooth smile. It was serene. Ancient.

"The woman with the two eyes," she whispered. "One storm. One sun."

She turned and skipped out of the room, humming a tune that sounded like the wind through a canyon.

William sat alone in the pool of light. The page was blank. But the ring... the ring was glowing.

CHAPTER 4

The Test of Stillness

William was early. He stood in front of Room 207C, his heart thumping like a tribal drum against his ribs, his palms sweating against the journal in his hoodie pocket. The hallway was empty, oddly silent, as if the air itself had stopped to listen.

The door didn't just open; it exhaled. A draft of cold air, scented with old paper and ozone, brushed past him as the heavy wood swung inward.

Inside, Professor Morrin stood beside the obsidian table, a glass jar in her hand.

"You came back," she said. It wasn't a question.

"Kind of hard to ignore glowing rings, mystery doors, and my little sister casually quoting you in her sleep."

"Ah. She's touched, that one. Touched by the Archive. Perhaps more than you."

William took a careful step inside. The room felt tighter today, the shadows stretching longer than the light sources allowed. "You said there was a test?"

Morrin nodded. "Yes. And it begins now."

She walked to a stone pedestal in the far corner and placed the jar on top. Inside was... nothing.

No, not nothing. Darkness. Contained, dense, and heavy, like a thought you couldn't unthink. It pulsed faintly, a heartbeat without a body.

"This," Morrin said, "is a Memory Unheard. A piece of silence that was never spoken, never written, and never allowed to exist."

"Okay," William said, his voice shaking slightly. "And I'm supposed to do what? Talk to it?"

"No. You must endure it."

"Endure what?"

"The urge to fill it."

Morrin stepped back, and the walls didn't only move, it shifted. The room folded inward, the bookshelves dissolving into mist, the floor dropping away into a vast, echoless void. Morrin blurred and vanished, leaving William standing on a suspended slice of reality.

Then, the noise stopped.

It wasn't just quiet. It was a vacuum. The silence pressed against his eardrums, heavy and physical. It demanded sound. It pulled at his throat, begging him to cough, to speak, to scream, anything to prove he still existed.

His heart hammered. The urge to say "Hello?" was a physical ache in his jaw.

Don't speak, he told himself. Listen.

He closed his eyes. He let the silence weigh him down. He felt the vibration of it in the marrow of his bones.

And then, the void cracked.

He wasn't in the dark anymore. He was standing in a memory, warm, humid, and scented with crushed spices and river mud. An open-air marketplace. Voices shouted in Swahili, laughing, bartering.

Men carved symbols into stone with rhythmic chink-chink-chink sounds. Women wove silence into cloth, their hands moving like water.

A boy stood nearby, no older than William. His skin was deep umber, his head shaved but for a single braid. In his hands was a scroll of bark. His lips moved, but no sound came out.

He turned, looked at William, and smiled.

"You're late," he said, not with sound, but with a thought. The voice resonated directly in William's chest.

"Where am I?" William thought back, instinctively realizing his mouth was useless here.

"You are in the First Forgetting. This is where it began."

The boy raised the scroll.

"The Seventh Silence was never lost. It was buried inside those who would listen."

"Buried where?"

The boy stepped forward and pressed his hand over William's heart. The touch was electric, a jolt of recognition that felt like remembering a name he'd known before he was born.

"Here."

The market dissolved like smoke in a gale. William gasped, his lungs seizing as reality rushed back in. The Archive reassembled around him, stone by stone, book by book.

He was in the room again. The jar sat on the pedestal, unbroken.

Professor Morrin stood unmoved, but her eyes shimmered, both the storm and the sun watching him closely. "You didn't speak."

William didn't answer. He couldn't. He reached into his hoodie, pulled out the journal, and drew the symbol from the vision. The spiral. The curve. The mark carved by silence.

Morrin looked at the drawing and smiled. A rare, sharp thing.

"Welcome, Keeper."

She opened a drawer and pulled out a map; old, worn, and pulsing faintly with gold thread. Dozens of places were marked in red. But seven were blacked out.

"Seven Silences," she said. "Six have broken. The Seventh is waking. And now it's looking for you."

"Why me?" William asked, his voice rasping.

She turned the map around and pointed to the bottom corner, where a name had been etched in ancient script and then erased.

Slowly, beneath her finger, the ink bled back into existence.

VALE.

"Because, William," Morrin said, "you were never meant to find the Archive. You were meant to be it."

CHAPTER 5

Jesse Knows Things He Shouldn't

William didn't sleep that night.

It wasn't for a lack of trying. He had lain there, tracing the cracks in the ceiling until they began to look like maps of countries that didn't exist. But every time his eyelids grew heavy, the symbol burned against the back of his eyes, a flash-bulb afterimage that refused to fade.

The spiral. The curve. The name that wasn't just a label, but an anchor. Vale.

By the time he dragged himself to school the next morning, the world felt abrasive. The squeak of sneakers on linoleum shrieked like tortured rubber; the slam of lockers echoed like gunfire in a canyon.

Jesse was waiting at his locker, guarding a box of cereal as if it were a holy relic.

"Bro," Jesse said, squinting at him. "You look like you summoned a demon, lost the negotiation, and then had to pay for its Uber."

"I didn't sleep."

"Because of the freaky note? The door that wasn't a door? The eye-lady who looks at you like you're a typo she wants to correct?"

"All of the above."

Jesse crunched a handful of dry loops, oblivious to the noise that made William wince. "You gonna let me in on it, or are we playing the 'brooding protagonist' card all week?"

William opened his mouth to deflect, then stopped. He hadn't told Jesse the specifics. He hadn't mentioned the glowing ring, the Memory Unheard, or the map where his name had been erased and rewritten.

And yet...

"Jesse," William said slowly, the fine hair on his arms standing up. "How do you know about the door?"

Jesse paused, a loop halfway to his mouth. "What do you mean? You told me."

"I didn't."

"Dude, yes you did. Yesterday. After class. You walked up to me and said..." Jesse's eyes glazed over for a split second, his voice flattening into a monotone drone that didn't belong to a sixteen-year-old boy. "'The door breathes when you touch it. The room is made of memory.'"

The air between them went frigid.

William stepped closer. "Jesse, I never said that out loud. I only thought it."

Jesse blinked, the color draining from his face. The playfulness vanished, replaced by a dawn of genuine fear. He rubbed his temples. "Wait. I... I remember you saying it. But I don't remember hearing it. Does that make sense? It's like..."

"Like a memory you didn't make," William finished.

Jesse looked at him, terrified. "Am I possessed? Please tell me I'm not possessed. I have a math test on Friday."

William didn't answer. He pulled his journal from his backpack, flipped to a fresh page, and sketched the spiral symbol, the one from the test, the one from his eyes wouldn't stop seeing.

"Have you seen this?"

Jesse didn't recoil. He didn't ask what it was. He just let out a long, shaky breath, his eyes locking onto the ink.

"It hums," Jesse whispered. "In my head. It sounds like... like a cello string snapping."

***

The transition from the chaos of the hallway to the suffocating quiet of Room 207C felt like stepping into an airlock. William didn't even remember walking there; one moment he was staring at a terrified Jesse, the next he was standing before the obsidian desk, recounting the incident while the smell of ozone filled his nose.

Professor Morrin listened to the account without blinking. She didn't look surprised; she looked resigned.

"Resonance leakage," she said, tapping a finger against the dark stone. "He has been in your orbit too long, Mr. Vale. You are a radio tower broadcasting on a frequency only the Archive uses. Your friend. .. has become an unintentional receiver."

"So, what do we do?" William asked, gripping the edge of the desk. "Is he in danger? Do we seal him off?"

"Distance won't help now. The connection is tethered." Morrin looked at him, her storm-eye clouding over. "We train him. Or rather, we teach him how to shield his mind. Because once someone is marked by the silence, they either awaken... or they shatter."

"He's not a Keeper. He's just a kid who likes bad cereal."

"The Archive does not care about his dietary habits, William. It cares that he is listening."

***

The walk home felt less like a commute and more like a trespass. The wind wasn't moving the leaves; it was moving through them. The shadows stretched toward William's feet like iron filings drawn to a magnet.

Jesse walked beside him, unusually quiet, kicking at a loose stone.

"So," Jesse said finally. "I'm a 'receiver'? What does that even mean? Do I get free cable? Or just nightmares?"

"Morrin thinks you can help."

"Help? I almost fainted when the lunch lady looked at me wrong last week."

"You're stronger than you think, Jess."

"Bold assumption."

They turned the corner onto 4th Street, passing the old brick retaining wall that bordered the park. It was covered in layers of graffiti: names, dates, crude drawings of anatomical impossibilities.

But as they passed, the graffiti stopped being paint.

William stopped. "Jesse. Look."

The spray paint was moving. The loops of letters and tags were uncoiling, sliding across the brick like liquid mercury. They pooled together, twisting and snapping until they formed a shape William recognized instantly.

The Seventh Silence.

But it wasn't glowing gold this time. It was burning black, scorching the brick.

"Uh, Will?" Jesse backed up, his voice trembling. "Why is the wall vibrating?"

It wasn't just vibrating. It was humming a low, nausea-inducing thrum that twisted William's belly. The symbol on the wall pulsed, and then, slowly, a new message burned itself into the mortar next to it.

HERETIC.

"Run," William whispered.

"Way ahead of you."

But before they could move, the humming stopped. The silence that followed was worse. It was absolute. The kind of silence that comes before a crash.

The brick wall didn't explode outward. It imploded.

With a sound like a cracking spine, the masonry folded inward, sucking the dust and debris into a void that hadn't been there a second ago. Where the wall had been, there was now a jagged hole.

And inside the hole, it wasn't a sewer. It wasn't a park. It was a tunnel, lined with torchlight that burned cold blue. And from the darkness, a voice, hoarse and old, drifted out to meet them.

"You are late, Keeper."

Jesse looked at the tunnel, then at William. "Okay. New rule. Next time a wall eats itself, we walk the other way."

William shook his head; the pull in his chest stronger than fear. It was the same pull he'd felt in the classroom, the same pull he felt in his dreams.

"We can't." He stepped toward the breach. "We're invited."

CHAPTER 6

The Tunnel of Forgotten Keepers

William stared into the abyss. It wasn't merely the absence of light; it was a physical weight, an ancient, suffocating darkness that felt like it had been holding its breath for centuries.

"Yeah, no," Jesse said, his voice hitching slightly. "That is horror-movie darkness. I've seen this film. The comic relief dies first, and I am very clearly the comic relief."

"You can stay here," William offered, though his own heart was trying to jump out of his chest every few seconds.

"And let you walk into this heaven-knows-what alone? Please. I'm an idiot, not heartless."

They stepped across the threshold.

The air shifted instantly. The chill of the evening vanished, replaced by a dry, static warmth. The walls were not brick or stone, but something organic, layers of compressed history, etched with symbols that pulsed with a faint, bioluminescent sorrow.

"What is this place?" Jesse whispered, no longer joking.

William ran his hand near the wall. He didn't touch it, yet he felt the vibration in his teeth. "A necropolis," he murmured. "But not for bodies. For voices."

The tunnel spilled them into a circular chamber, perfectly symmetrical and terrifyingly silent. Seven pillars rose to the vaulted ceiling, though one had been shattered, not by time, but by violence. The jagged stump of the seventh pillar looked raw, as if the stone were still bleeding.

Behind the ruin stood a wall of names. Thousands of them, scratched into the obsidian surface in scripts William didn't know but instinctively read.

Vale

Ashem.

Elian

Chuma.

And below them all, gouged deep enough to scar the rock: The Heretic.

The air suddenly pressurized, popping their ears. A cold wind, smelling of ash and thunderstorms, swept through the stagnant room. The wall seemed to inhale.

- A voice, genderless, ageless, and everywhere at once, vibrated from the stone itself.

"The Seventh was not lost. He was silenced."

Jesse scrambled back, tripping over his own feet. "Did the wall just fact-check us?"

"I don't know," William whispered, unable to look away from the gouged name.

"Well, maybe tell it you're just a seventh grader who is barely passing algebra and is not emotionally equipped for ancestral grievances!"

But William wasn't listening. That pull in his chest, the one that felt like a hook snagging his heart, was dragging him toward the back of the chamber.

A section of the obsidian wall dissolved, melting away like ink in water. Standing in the newly revealed recess was a figure. At first, he seemed made of shadow and dust, but as he stepped into the faint light of the glowing symbols, he solidified.

He wore robes stitched with impossible geometries, and his eyes were pools of absolute black.

"You are not supposed to be here," the figure said. His voice was calm, the terrible calm of a man who has watched empires burn.

"Who are you?" William asked, his voice trembling.

"I was a Keeper once."

"You're… one of them? From the Archive?"

"No," the figure corrected softly. "I was the first to refuse it."

He stepped closer. The air around him distorted, rippling with heat. "I am what happens when memory is weaponized."

William felt his feet root to the floor. Beside him, Jesse was hyperventilating quietly.

"The Seventh Silence is not what you think," the man continued. "You believe it is a mystery? A secret? No. It is an amputation. It is the deliberate removal of truth to preserve power. And someone is trying to stitch the limb back on."

He turned his gaze to Jesse. The boy froze.

"And you… you are a crack in the glass. You were never meant to hold this resonance."

"Okay, rude," Jesse squeaked. "I have many redeeming qualities."

The ground beneath them groaned. It wasn't the sound of stone breaking; it was the sound of a lock turning.

Suddenly, the symbols on the walls flared. Not the gentle gold of the Archive, but a violent, arterial crimson. They surged up the pillars like climbing vines of fire.

"You've brought the Archive with you," the Heretic hissed, backing away into the shadows. "It is already leaking through your skin."

William stepped in front of Jesse, shielding him. "Tell us how to stop it!"

The man looked at him, a look of infinite pity. "You don't stop the flood, boy. You either learn to breathe underwater… or you drown."

The floor didn't just collapse; it vanished.

Gravity reclaimed them. They fell—not into the dark, but through it.

When William opened his eyes, the world had inverted. He was lying on a surface that felt like glass, suspended in a void. Jesse was groaning beside him, clutching his stomach.

"Tell me we're not dead," Jesse wheezed. "Because if this is the afterlife, the decor is very disappointing."

"Not yet," William said, sitting up.

He froze.

Floating around them, suspended in the chamber's anti-gravity, were hundreds of scrolls. But they weren't rolled up. They were unfurled, glowing with a starlight that didn't exist.

William looked up at the one hovering inches above his face. It depicted a painting that moved; a boy standing between two worlds, a ring on his finger, and seven eyes watching from a tearing sky.

At the bottom, written in a language that burned his eyes to read, were three words:

The Seventh Returns.

CHAPTER 7

The Girl Who Didn't Look Away

The fall didn't end with a crash; it ended with a hiccup in reality.

One moment, gravity was dragging them into a suffocating abyss of ancient stone and cold air. The next, the sensation of falling simply... deleted itself.

William gasped, his heels hitting the floor hard enough to jar his teeth. But it wasn't rock beneath him. It was polished wood. And the air wasn't stale; it smelled of chalk dust and floor wax.

He scrambled to his feet, eyes darting wildly.

They were back in Room 207C. The obsidian table in its perfect position at the center. The shelves of scrolls stood in perfect, silent rows.

Beside him, Jesse was crouched on all fours, hyperventilating. He stared at the floor, then at the ceiling, then back at the floor.

"No," Jesse said, shaking his head. "Nope. I refuse."

"Jesse, we're—"

"Don't say it," Jesse snapped, his voice pitching high. "We were in a tunnel. Underground. Deep underground. This is the second floor of the school. I know this because I hate the stairs. You cannot fall down and land up. That is negative math. That is broken physics."

"Distance is relative here," a voice said.

Professor Morrin stood by the blackboard, her hands clasped behind her back. She looked unruffled, as if students dropping from the ceiling was a standard Tuesday occurrence.

Jesse pointed a trembling finger at her. "You. You did this. You broke the map."

"Mr. Tran," Morrin said, her tone sounding bored. "You are leaking tunnel dust onto my floor."

"I'm leaking dust? I'm leaking sanity! We just teleported!"

"You traversed," she corrected. She walked to the classroom door and held it open. The sounds of the hallway drifted in lockers banging, laughter, the squeak of sneakers. It was aggressively, violently normal.

"Out," she said simply.

"Out?" Jesse sputtered. "You can't just kick me out after I fell through a plot hole!"

"Mr. Tran, you are currently experiencing a collision between memory and reality. If you stay in this room, your brain will try to reconcile the two, and you will likely pass out. If you walk into that hallway, you will see a vending machine and forget this ever happened." She gestured to the hall. "I suggest you choose the vending machine."

Jesse scrambled to his feet, dusting off his jeans. He looked at William. "Dude. We are talking about this. We are having a debrief. A PowerPoint presentation may be required."

"Go, Jesse. I'll find you," William said quietly, his eyes fixed on Morrin. "I need to talk to her."

Jesse hesitated, looking between the impossible teacher and his best friend. "Okay. Fine. I'm getting a soda. But if I turn into a newt, I'm suing the school district."

He bolted into the hallway. Morrin shut the door with a click that felt final.

William stood alone with her.

The fear was gone now, replaced by a cold clarity that settled in his chest. He looked at the woman who had handed him a ring, opened a door, and threw him into a history he hadn't asked for.

"You lied to me," William said, his voice scraping against the silence.

"About what?"

"The Seventh Silence. The Heretic. That I was supposed to find the Archive. That I am the Archive."

"I didn't lie," she said calmly. "I... curated."

"That's the same thing."

"No, William. That is how knowledge works. You don't pour boiling water into a paper cup. You wait until the vessel has hardened."

"I'm not a cup."

"No," she said, a faint, dangerous smile touching her lips. "You are the fire."

    ***

The rest of the school day passed in a blur of mundane noise. Lockers slammed with jarring cheerfulness. Students complained about math tests and the impending gym class. It felt like watching a movie with the sound out of sync.

William didn't speak to Jesse again until lunch, but even then, words felt inadequate. They walked through the halls like ghosts haunting their own lives.

That was when he saw her.

Amaya Reyes.

She sat on the edge of the courtyard fountain, the wind catching her dark curls. She wasn't reading her history textbook; she was defacing it. A thick black marker moved across the page, striking out line after line of text with surgical precision.

He didn't know how long he'd been staring until Jesse bumped him with a sharp elbow.

"Go."

"What?"

"You've been pining after her since sixth grade. And unless she's secretly a time-traveling archivist of forbidden truth—which, given your week, is statistically probable—this might be your last chance at a normal conversation."

William took a breath and walked over like he was approaching a cliff edge.

"Hey," he said.

"Hey, Vale," Amaya said, not looking up. Her marker squeaked as she redacted a paragraph about the Industrial Revolution. "You look like you crawled out of a collapsed mine shaft."

"I... sort of did."

She paused, marker hovering. She looked up, her eyes dark and sharply intelligent. "...What?"

"Nothing. Uh, just—bad morning."

"You mean yesterday's mysterious substitute who wrote in hieroglyphs? Or the fact that the brick wall near the gym spontaneously combusted into a hallway that doesn't exist?"

William blinked. "You saw that?"

"Of course I saw it. People think because I don't talk, I don't see." She capped her marker with a definitive click. "They notice the noise. I notice the edits."

She stood, clutching her censored book to her chest.

"I know what you're trying to do," she said, stepping closer.

"You do?"

"You're trying to find logic in the glitch. But it won't make sense, William. Not yet." She lowered her voice, her gaze locking onto his. "But when the world starts talking to you, the walls, the wind, the pages that rewrite themselves? Listen."

William's stomach did a slow somersault. "Are you saying you—"

"I'm saying this: you're not crazy, and you're not alone." She pressed a folded slip of paper into his hand. "Read this tonight. And don't trust everything Morrin says."

She turned on her heel and walked away, her combat boots silent on the pavement.

"Wait—how do you know Morrin?" William called out.

"I don't," she said over her shoulder. "But I know a gatekeeper when I see one."

***

That night, the silence in William's room felt heavy, pregnant with things unsaid. He sat at his desk and unfolded Amaya's note.

Inside, there was a symbol, not the spiral of the Archive, nor the jagged mark of the Heretic. It was something else. Something architectural.

And beneath it, in handwriting that was sharp and unyielding:

"They've lied before. Even to themselves.

The Archive is not a library.

It's a weapon."

CHAPTER 8

The Symbol Lilith Drew

William woke to the sound of friction—wax dragging heavy across paper.

He sat up, his heart doing a double-beat against his ribs. The room was dark, save for the sliver of hallway light that cut across the floor like a caution tape.

Lilith sat at the foot of his bed. She was cross-legged, a red crayon gripped in her fist like a dagger, attacking a sheet of printer paper on her lap.

"Lil?" he whispered, his voice thick with sleep. "What are you doing?"

"It's too loud," she murmured. She didn't look up. Her hand moved in jerky, violent spasms. "I have to put it down so it stops talking."

William slid off the mattress, the floorboards cold against his bare feet. He crouched beside her, expecting to see a nightmare drawn in wax, monsters, teeth, storm clouds.

It wasn't a monster. It was geometry.

The page was covered in symbols—jagged, recursive shapes that looked less like drawing and more like scarring. And in the center, dominating the white space, was a single, complex glyph. It looked like the Archive's spiral, but inverted, fractured, and pulled inside out.

It hurt to look at. Not physically, but mentally. His brain slid off the shape, unable to find a purchase.

"Where did you see this?" William asked, his throat dry.

Lilith stopped. The crayon hovered millimeters from the paper.

"I didn't see it," she said, turning to him. Her eyes were wide, but the pupils were pinpricks. "I heard it."

"You... heard a drawing?"

"It remembers the lies, Will," she whispered. "It remembers all of them."

***

The next morning, the school cafeteria smelled of disinfectant and hopelessness. Jesse slid a glazed donut across the table. It left a greasy streak on the laminate.

"Eat," Jesse commanded. "You look like you've been haunting a Victorian mansion for three centuries and just found out they're turning it into a condo."

William stared at the donut. "Lilith drew something last night. Symbols."

"Kids draw weird stuff, man. My cousin once drew a potato and said it was God. We still don't talk about it."

"This wasn't a potato. It was... architecture. Complex. Ancient. And she said she 'heard' it."

Jesse paused, a chunk of donut halfway to his mouth. He lowered it slowly. "Heard it? Like you hear the library-that-isn't-there?"

"Exactly like that."

Jesse grimaced. "Okay. That upgrades this from 'creepy kid stuff' to 'generational curse.' Do we need an exorcist? Or just a really good eraser?"

"I need Morrin," William said, standing up.

"Right. The eye-lady. Because she's definitely the person to ask about cursed crayon art. Good luck. If you don't come back, can I have your stereo?"

"I don't have a stereo."

"Then get one. And leave it to me in your will."

***

Room 207C did not welcome him.

The moment William stepped through the door, the air pressure dropped. The floating motes of dust froze in place.

He walked to the obsidian table and slapped the piece of printer paper down. The red wax looked violent against the black stone.

"Explain this," he demanded.

Professor Morrin looked down. For a long moment, she didn't move. Then, very slowly, she reached out a hand. Her fingers hovered over the paper, trembling.

The gray eye and the gold eye both widened.

"Where did you get this?" Her voice was barely a whisper.

"My sister. She drew it last night."

"She drew it?" Morrin looked up, and for the first time, William saw fear. Not concern. Fear. "She shouldn't be able to conceive of this structure. No human mind should."

"She said she heard it."

Morrin pulled her hand back as if the paper had burned her. She turned to the shelves, her cane clicking sharply on the floor. She bypassed the scrolls, the books, the maps. She went to a small, sealed cabinet at the far back, secured with a lock that had no keyhole.

She placed her palm against it. The lock hissed and clicked open.

She pulled out a slate tablet, cracked down the middle.

"We called it the Unwritten Word," she said, placing the tablet next to Lilith's drawing.

The symbol carved into the stone was identical to the one in red crayon.

"It predates the Silences," Morrin said, her voice hollow. "It is a language of absolute truth. It cannot be spoken, because to speak it is to unmake the reality that contradicts it. It was banned. Erased. Buried beneath seven layers of silence."

"Then how does my six-year-old sister know it?"

Morrin looked at the drawing, then at William.

"Because," she said softly, "the Archive is leaking. And the leak is flowing downstream to the youngest mind it can find."

"How do I stop it?"

"You don't stop an avalanche, William," Morrin said, her eyes grim. "You try to survive the fall."

***

That night, William sat in the hallway outside Lilith's room, keeping watch. The house was quiet, but it was a heavy quiet, the kind that holds its breath.

Inside, Lilith stirred.

"She's coming," a small voice murmured.

William froze. He leaned into the doorway. "Who, Lil? Who's coming?"

Lilith sat up in bed. Her eyes were closed, but she turned her head unerringly toward him.

"The one who broke the First Silence," she whispered.

She opened her eyes. They weren't her eyes. They were glowing with a faint, terrible silver light.

"And William?" the voice said, not Lilith's voice, but something older, layered like a choir of ghosts.

"She remembers you."

CHAPTER 9

The Chamber of Unspoken Histories

William had never seen Professor Morrin pace before. She was a figure of stillness, exuding statuesque authority. But now, she moved back and forth behind her obsidian desk like a trapped animal, the hem of her robes kicking up small clouds of dust.

"The Unwritten Word was a theory," she muttered, more to herself than to him. "A philosophical exercise. It wasn't supposed to be... accessible."

"But now my sister is drawing it with Crayola," William said, leaning against the doorframe. "You said it predates the Archive. What does that mean?"

Morrin stopped. She turned to him, and the light in the room seemed to dim, pulling shadows into the hollows of her face.

"The Archive was built to preserve truth," she said. "But to preserve something, you must first define it. You must decide what is true and what isn't."

"Okay..."

"Before the Archive, there was no filter. No curation. There was only the raw, chaotic noise of everything that ever happened. We call that the Chaos. But the Echoes? They call it the Truth."

"So the Archive is…"

"A filter," she whispered. "And if your sister is hearing what's outside the filter… then the walls are thinner than I thought."

Suddenly, a sound cut through the room, a high-pitched whine, like a hearing test gone wrong. The lanterns on the wall flickered, their flames turning a sickly, static gray before flaring gold again.

Morrin looked up, her expression tightening. "It's starting."

***

That night, sleep was a stranger who refused to visit.

William lay in bed, staring at the ceiling, but all he could see was the inverted spiral Lilith had drawn. It burned in his mind, a glowing afterimage of something wrong.

Around 2:00 AM, the pull started.

It wasn't a voice this time. It was a physical sensation, a tug behind his sternum, like a hook caught on a rib, pulling him upright. Pulling him out.

He didn't fight it. He pulled on his sneakers and hoodie, slipping out of the house like a shadow. The streets were empty, washed in the sodium-orange glow of streetlights. But something felt off. The street sign on the corner was blank. Just a green rectangle. He blinked, and the letters ELM STREET flickered back into existence.

Just tired, he told himself. Just tired.

Room 207C opened before he even touched the handle.

But this wasn't the classroom.

The walls had dissolved. The ceiling was gone, replaced by a void of swirling, silent stars. He was standing on a walkway of translucent stone, suspended over an abyss of whispering light.

Floating panels of glass drifted past him like icebergs in a dark sea. Each one held a scene, a moving, living memory. But they were damaged. A memory of a burning library skipped and repeated like a scratched DVD. A scene of a coronation was blurred, the king's face pixelated into static.

And then, he saw the tree.

It wasn't a plant. It was a genealogy, vast and glowing, projected in the air like a hologram. The roots were deep, tangled in history. The branches reached up toward the present.

He found his own branch.

Celeste Vale.

Mira Elian Vale.

Amari Ashem Vale.

The names glowed with a steady, golden warmth. His lineage. The Keepers.

But as he watched, a ripple distorted the air. It looked like heat haze, shimmering and warping the light.

The name Amari Ashem Vale flickered. It turned static-gray, then dissolved into code, scrambled symbols that meant nothing.

In its place, a new name carved itself into the light. The letters were sharp, jagged, and cold.

Jhalia Vynn.

William stepped back, his breath hitching. "No," he whispered. "That's not... that's not right."

The ripple moved up the tree. It hit his grandmother's name. Mira Elian Vale vanished. Replaced by Mira Vynn.

It was climbing. It was rewriting.

And then it reached him.

William Vale.

The name turned red. It didn't vanish. It pulsed, fighting the change. The letters vibrated violently, the red light bleeding into the gold, resisting the rewrite.

"You shouldn't be seeing this."

The voice came from behind him. William spun around, nearly slipping on the translucent stone.

Amaya stood there. She wasn't wearing her school uniform; she was dressed in black, her arms crossed, her expression grim.

"Amaya? How did you—"

"They're rewriting you, Will," she said, her voice devoid of its usual sarcasm. She walked past him, looking at the glitching family tree. "They're cutting the roots so the tree dies."

"Who?"

"The ones who want to bring back the Seventh Silence. The Curators who think the Archive has become too soft." She pointed at the blank street sign in his memory, the one he had just seen outside. "It starts with names. Then street signs. Then entire days."

She turned to him, her face illuminated by the red pulsing light of his own threatened name.

"They can't kill you, William. You're too connected to the source. So they're doing the next best thing."

"They're changing who I came from," William realized, a cold horror settling in his gut.

"If they change your past," Amaya said, "they change your loyalty. If you descend from Jhalia Vynn, the Great Betrayer, then you don't belong to the Keepers. You belong to the Silence."

She stepped closer, her eyes intense.

"You're not just part of the Archive, Will,' she said. 'You're the last original memory it has."

And if they can erase you...they can erase everything. They can erase the truth.".

CHAPTER 10

The Name Lilith Shouldn't Know

The walk home felt like walking through a jpeg that hadn't fully loaded.

William kept blinking, expecting the world to glitch again—for a mailbox to vanish or a parked car to turn into a horse-drawn carriage. But the street remained stubbornly normal. The only thing wrong was the silence. It wasn't empty; it was heavy, pressing against his eardrums like deep water.

He slipped through his front door, locking it behind him. The click of the deadbolt usually made him feel safe. Tonight, it just felt like locking himself inside a trap.

He started down the hallway toward his room, passing the family photo gallery.

His mom loved that wall. It was a chaotic collage of framed moments: birthdays, graduations, beach trips. William had walked past it a thousand times. He knew every image by heart.

He stopped.

His eyes snagged on a black-and-white photo of his great-grandmother, Amari. In his memory, she was standing in front of a library, holding a thick, leather-bound book.

He looked at the photo.

She was still standing in front of the library. But she wasn't holding a book.

She was holding a torch.

William blinked, rubbing his eyes hard. He looked again. The torch was still there, the flame captured in grainy grayscale. And the expression on her face... it wasn't the gentle smile he remembered. It was hard. Defiant.

"No," he whispered.

He reached out to touch the frame. The glass was cold, but the paper inside seemed to hum against his fingertips.

They're rewriting you.

He pulled his hand back. If the photo had changed, what else? The birth certificates in the safe? The stories his mom told him about where they came from?

A sound drifted from down the hall. A low, rhythmic murmuring.

Lilith.

William moved away from the wall, his heart hammering. He pushed open Lilith's door.

She was sitting up in bed, her eyes wide open but unseeing, staring at a corner of the room where nothing existed. Her hands were folded in her lap, fingers knotted together so tightly her knuckles were white.

"...Zahren-Tai," she whispered, her voice devoid of inflection. "Vehlur Ossah. Yis'Ketra."

She was reciting names.

"Lil?" William stepped into the room. The air smelled sharp, like burning hair.

"...Jhalia Vynn," Lilith said.

47

The name hit William like a physical blow.

"Lilith, stop."

"Jhalia Vynn," she repeated, louder this time. "Born of the Seventh. Keeper of the ash. Mother of the betrayal."

William rushed to the bed and grabbed her shoulders. "Lilith! Wake up!"

She didn't blink. Her head turned toward him, mechanical and smooth. Her eyes were still that terrifying, glowing silver.

"The tree is rotting, William," she said. The voice wasn't hers. It was deeper, layered with the dust of centuries. "They are cutting the roots. If you do not claim the soil, you will fall."

"Who are you?" William demanded.

Lilith blinked. The silver faded, replaced by her own warm brown eyes. She slumped forward, collapsing into William's arms.

"Will?" she whimpered, sounding tiny and six years old again. "My head hurts. It's too full."

William held her, rocking her back and forth. "I know, munchkin. I know."

He looked over her shoulder at the wall. Lilith had drawn on it.

In red crayon, scrawled across the floral wallpaper, was a family tree. But the names weren't his ancestors. They were strangers. And at the bottom, where his name should have been, she had written:

THE REMINDER.

***

"You knew," William said.

He didn't yell. He didn't have the energy for it. He stood in front of Morrin's desk the next morning, the red-crayon drawing of the family tree crumpled in his fist.

Morrin didn't look up from her grading. "Good morning, Mr. Vale. Please lower your voice. The scrolls are sensitive to aggression."

"My great-grandmother is holding a torch in the photo now," William said, slamming his hand on the desk. "She used to hold a book. And my sister—my six-year-old sister—is chanting the name of a woman who didn't exist yesterday."

Morrin stopped writing. She set her pen down, aligning it perfectly with the edge of the paper.

"Jhalia Vynn," she said softly.

"Who is she?"

"A fiction," Morrin said, looking up. "A narrative device inserted into your bloodline. If they can make you believe you are descended from a traitor, they believe you will act like one."

"But the photo changed, Morrin! The physical photo!"

"Yes. That is what the Rewrite does. It doesn't just change perception; it alters evidence. It changes the ink on the page, the pixels on the screen, the emulsion on the film."

William stared at her. "Then how do we fight it? If they can change reality, how do we win?"

Morrin stood up. She walked around the desk and stopped in front of him.

"Why do you think the Rewrite hasn't touched you yet, William?"

"Because I'm… what? The Keeper?"

"No. There have been many Keepers. They were all rewritten or erased." She leaned in closer. "You are not just a Keeper, William. You are the Control Group."

"I'm a what?"

"In every experiment, you need a baseline. A standard that does not change, so you can measure the deviation of everything else." She tapped his chest, right over his heart. "The Archive cannot rewrite itself entirely unless it has a reference point. A backup drive. Someone who remembers the original version so the system doesn't collapse into chaos."

William felt a chill slide down his spine. "I'm the backup."

"You are the Original Memory," Morrin said. "You are the only thing in this world that cannot be edited. As long as you remember the truth, the Rewrite is just a layer of paint over the wall. But if you forget…"

"Then the paint becomes the wall," William finished.

"Exactly." Morrin's eyes were fierce. "They are attacking your history because they cannot touch your mind. They want you to doubt who you are. Because if you accept the lie… then the lie becomes the truth."

She turned back to the blackboard, where a map of the school was drawn in chalk.

"Go to class, Mr. Vale. And when you look at that photo of your grandmother? Remember the book. Don't just think it. See it. Force the world to blink before you do."

CHAPTER 11

The Prophecy That Knew His Name

The school was hemorrhaging reality.

It wasn't obvious to everyone else. The other students navigated the hallways like nothing was wrong, laughing at jokes and slamming locker doors. But William could see the seams splitting.

A poster for the "Fall Dance" flickered and became a poster for a "Spring Carnival" before snapping back. The clock on the wall jumped from 10:15 to 2:00, then back to 10:16. The PA system crackled, broadcasting a few seconds of a language that sounded like Latin spoken backward before the Vice Principal's voice returned to announce pizza day.

William kept his head down, gripping his backpack straps until his knuckles turned white. He hadn't slept properly in three days. The circles under his eyes felt like bruises.

I am the Control Group, he repeated mentally. I am the backup drive.

He found Jesse at their usual table in the cafeteria. It was Friday, which meant "Potato Surprise." Jesse was staring at a tray of tater tots with deep, philosophical suspicion.

"Safe," William breathed, sliding into the seat opposite him.

"Is it?" Jesse poked a tot. "These look radioactive. I think they glow in the dark."

William forced a laugh. It sounded brittle. "Better than the meat cubes from Monday, though. You still haven't recovered from watching me eat that tower."

Jesse looked up, his brow furrowing. "The what?"

"The meat cubes," William said. "The Jenga tower? Monday? You dared me to eat three of them. I did it, and you stood on the table and announced me as 'William the Indigestible.'"

Jesse laughed, but his eyes were blank. "Bro, what are you talking about? I've never seen you eat a meat cube in your life. You're a vegetarian."

The noise in the cafeteria seemed to drop away.

"Jesse," William said slowly, a cold knot forming in his stomach. "I'm not a vegetarian. And it was Monday. Four days ago. You were laughing so hard you snorted milk."

Jesse shook his head, looking genuinely confused. "Will, I think the stress is getting to you. I was out sick on Monday. Remember? Strep throat. I didn't come back until Wednesday."

William froze.

He remembered Monday. He remembered the smell of the mystery meat. He remembered the sound of Jesse's applause. It happened. It was the start of everything.

But looking at Jesse now, at the absolute, unshakeable certainty in his eyes, William felt a crack form in his own chest.

It's happening. It's rewriting him.

"Yeah," William whispered, his voice trembling. "Right. You were sick. My bad."

"You okay, man? You look wrecked." Jesse reached out.

William stood up abruptly. "I... I need air."

He turned and walked away. He didn't run, but he wanted to. He needed to find something solid. Something true.

He crashed into Amaya near the recycling bins.

"Watch it," she snapped, steadying him. Then she saw his face. Her expression shifted instantly from annoyance to alarm. "What happened?"

"Jesse," William choked out. "He forgot Monday. He was there, Amaya. But now he remembers being sick. He thinks I'm a vegetarian."

Amaya grabbed his arm and pulled him into the shadow of a stairwell. "The Rewrite is accelerating. It's moving from historical data to short-term memory."

"He looked at me like I was crazy," William said, clutching his hair. "If he forgets Monday... how long until he forgets me?"

"We don't have time for panic," Amaya said, her voice hard. "We need to go to the Codex."

"The what?"

"The hard drive," she said. "Morrin calls it a myth. I call it the only thing that remembers better than you do."

***

The school was silent after hours. Not just empty, but hollow, as if the building itself was holding its breath.

Amaya led him through a series of hallways that William was certain shouldn't connect. They went down a staircase in the science wing, took a left through the boiler room, and ended up in a corridor made of brick that smelled of damp earth and ozone.

"Where are we?" William whispered.

"Beneath the foundation," Amaya said.

She stopped at a dead end. The wall was blank brick. Amaya didn't look for a handle. She placed her hand flat against the center of the wall and closed her eyes.

"You have to ask it nicely," she murmured.

The bricks didn't move. They shivered. The mortar liquefied, turning into ink that ran down the wall, and the bricks folded inward like origami paper.

Behind the wall was a spiral staircase that went down into the dark.

"You've done this before?" William asked.

"Once," she said. "I wasn't supposed to. Curators aren't allowed to see the raw data."

They descended. The air grew colder, heavy with the static charge of a thunderstorm about to break.

At the bottom, the staircase opened into a circular chamber.

It wasn't a library. It was a root cellar.

Massive, glowing roots hung from the ceiling, pulsing with white light. They twisted together in the center of the room to form a rough, organic podium. And resting on that podium was the Codex.

It wasn't a book. It was a slab of obsidian, its surface shifting and rippling like liquid mercury.

"The Codex of Forgotten Truths," Amaya whispered. "It connects to the roots of the Archive. It records everything the Curators delete."

William stepped closer. The light from the roots cast long, dancing shadows on the walls.

"What do I do?"

"Touch it," Amaya said. "Ask it for the prophecy."

William reached out. His hand hovered over the liquid black surface.

I am the Control Group.

He pressed his palm down.

FLASH.

The room vanished.

William was standing on a battlefield of ash. The sky was torn open, bleeding red light. He saw a woman—*Jhalia Vynn*—holding a sword that wasn't made of metal, but of silence. She swung it, and where it cut, the world simply ceased to exist.

He saw a baby crying in a cradle of stone, but no sound came out.

He saw himself, older, scarred, standing on a mountain of burning books, holding a ring that shone like a dying star. And above him, seven eyes opened in the sky.

'The Seventh returns', a voice thundered, not in his ears, but in his blood. 'The One Who Remembers will burn or bloom. He will carry the First Voice. He will unwrite the lie.'

William gasped, yanking his hand back. He fell to his knees on the dirt floor of the chamber, gasping for air. The vision faded, but the words burned in his mind.

"What did you see?" Amaya was beside him, gripping his shoulder.

William looked up at her, his eyes wide.

"It showed me the end," he whispered. "And it called me the One Who Remembers."

The liquid surface of the Codex stopped rippling. It froze. Then, slowly, words began to carve themselves into the stone, glowing with a violent red light.

THEY HAVE FOUND ME.

The chamber shook. Dust rained down from the ceiling.

"What does that mean?" William scrambled back.

Amaya looked at the message, her face pale.

"It means," she said, "that by asking the question... we just alerted the answer."

CHAPTER 12

The Archive Is Lying

The Codex didn't just shake the room; it tried to digest it.

The glowing white roots hanging from the ceiling turned a violent, bruised purple. They uncoiled from the ceiling like waking snakes, lashing out at the space where William and Amaya stood.

"Run!" Amaya screamed.

She didn't have to tell him twice. William scrambled backward as a root the thickness of a fire hose slammed into the dirt exactly where he'd been kneeling. The impact didn't sound like wood hitting earth; it sounded like a wet thud of meat on bone.

"It's a security protocol!" Amaya yelled, shoving him toward the spiral staircase. "We triggered the immune system!"

The walls of the chamber began to bleed. Thick, black ink oozed from the mortar of the bricks, pooling on the floor and rising fast.

William hit the stairs, his sneakers slipping on the slick stone. He hauled himself up, grabbing the iron railing. Below them, the ink was rising like floodwater, swallowing the podium. The Codex sank beneath the surface, but the red words—THEY HAVE FOUND ME—burned through the black liquid like neon.

"Don't look back!" Amaya commanded.

They sprinted up the spiral, lungs burning. The air grew thinner, colder. The stone steps vibrated under their feet, threatening to crumble into dust.

At the top, the brick wall had folded itself shut again. Amaya didn't stop. She slammed her shoulder into the bricks.

"Open!" she shouted. Not a request this time. A command.

The wall hesitated, then burst outward, vomiting them onto the linoleum floor of the school hallway.

William skidded to a halt, gasping, his chest heaving. He looked back. The wall was solid brick again. No seam. No door. Just a poster advertising the Chess Club.

"What... was... that?" he wheezed.

"That," Amaya said, wiping black dust from her face, "was the truth fighting back."

"Guys?"

A voice drifted from down the hall. Jesse was standing by the janitor's closet, holding a mop bucket he definitely shouldn't have had access to. He stared at them, dusty, sweating, and terrified.

"I was looking for the bathroom," Jesse said, his voice trembling. "Why did you guys just explode out of a wall?"

William stood up, his legs shaking. "Jesse... you saw that?"

Jesse blinked. He looked at the wall. Then at William. Then back at the wall.

"I..." Jesse's brow furrowed. The certainty in his eyes wavered. "I saw... you guys were just... standing there. Talking about chess. Right?"

William felt his heart sink. The Rewrite was working fast. It was patching the glitch in Jesse's mind before the memory could even settle.

"Yeah," Amaya stepped in, her voice sharp. "Chess. We're very passionate about pawns. Go home, Jesse."

"Right. Chess." Jesse rubbed his temples. "I'm gonna go lie down. The air in here tastes like static."

He wandered off, leaving the mop bucket in the middle of the hall.

***

Room 207C was waiting for them.

When they entered, Professor Morrin wasn't grading papers. She was standing in the center of the room, her hands resting on the obsidian table. The map of the Archive was spread out, glowing with angry red nodes.

"You pinged the server," she said. Her voice was ice.

"We went to the Codex," William admitted.

Morrin looked at Amaya. "You violated your oath, Curator."

"I fulfilled it," Amaya shot back, stepping forward. "The oath is to preserve the truth. Not to hide it because it's inconvenient."

"The Codex is not truth!" Morrin slammed her hand on the table. "The Codex is raw, unverified data! It is the chaos we built the Archive to contain! It doesn't tell stories, Amaya. It screams facts without context!"

"It told me a name," William interrupted.

The room went silent. Morrin turned slowly to look at him.

"What name?"

"Jhalia Vynn," William said. "And it called me 'The One Who Remembers.'"

Morrin closed her eyes. She looked suddenly very old. She gripped the edge of the table, her knuckles white.

"Then it's too late," she whispered. "If the Codex has named you, then the Rewrite knows exactly where you are."

"Who is Jhalia Vynn?" William asked. "Is she my ancestor?"

"She is the Anti-Keeper," Morrin said, opening her eyes. "She was the first to realize that if you control the Archive, you don't just record history. You can edit it. She wanted to weaponize memory. We erased her. We buried her name so deep we thought it would never surface."

"But the Rewrite brought her back," Amaya said.

"No," Morrin said grimly. "The Rewrite is her."

***

William walked home in a daze. The world felt thin, like paper stretched too tight.

When he got to his house, the lights were flickering. Not just the bulbs, the electricity itself seemed to be pulsing in time with a heartbeat.

He went straight to his room.

Lilith was waiting.

She stood in the center of his rug, holding a small, smooth stone in her hand. She wasn't chanting this time. She looked calm. Terrifyingly calm.

"She's here, Will," Lilith said.

"Who is here?"

"The lady from the tree. Jhalia."

William locked his bedroom door, as if a deadbolt could stop a reality-warping sorceress. "Where is she, Lil?"

Lilith held out the stone. It was dark gray, etched with a single eye that seemed to be closed.

"She's not in the house," Lilith whispered. "She's in the ink."

"The ink?"

"The pictures, Will. The letters. The things written down." Lilith pressed the stone into his hand. It was cold. "She lives in the things we trust to remember for us."

The stone in William's hand suddenly grew warm. The closed eye carved into its surface snapped open.

And from downstairs, he heard his mother scream.

CHAPTER 13

The Echoes Do Not Whisper

William didn't run down the stairs; he fell down them.

"Mom!"

He skidded into the kitchen, his heart hammering like a trapped bird. The room was empty. A pot of pasta water was boiling over on the stove, the hiss of steam the only sound in the house.

"Mom?"

He checked the living room. The den. The backyard. Nothing.

He found her in the laundry room. She was standing in front of the washing machine, staring blankly at the spinning drum. Her mouth was open in a silent scream, but her eyes were glazed over, as if she were watching a nightmare projected on the inside of her skull.

"Mom!" William grabbed her shoulders. She was freezing cold.

She blinked, and the scream died in her throat. She looked at him, her eyes unfocused.

"William?" she whispered. "I... I forgot."

"Forgot what?"

"I forgot where I was. I forgot... who I was." She touched her face, trembling. "For a second, the world just... went gray. Like a TV channel with no signal."

William hugged her, holding her tight. Over her shoulder, he saw the box of detergent on the dryer. The logo, a bright blue wave, flickered. For a split second, it became a jagged, red eye.

She's in the ink, Lilith had said. She lives in the things we trust to remember for us.

"I'm here, Mom," William said, his voice fierce. "I'm here. We're okay."

But they weren't. And he knew it.

***

"We have to go underground," Amaya said.

They were back at the school, standing by the fountain, easily her favorite spot. It was dark now, the campus abandoned.

"We already went underground," William said, pacing. "We found the Codex. We triggered the alarm. My mom almost got deleted in her own laundry room, Amaya. I'm done with underground."

"Not the Codex," she said. "Deeper."

She led him not to a door, but to the maintenance shed behind the football field. Inside, amidst the smell of gasoline and cut grass, she pulled aside a tarp to reveal a grate.

"The Archive has layers," she said, pulling the grate open. "The Classroom is the interface. The Codex is the hard drive. But this?" She pointed into the darkness. "This is the Recycle Bin."

They climbed down.

This tunnel wasn't like the others. It didn't smell of ozone or magic. It smelled of wet earth and copper. The walls were rough, unpolished stone, covered in graffiti. But as William looked closer, he realized it wasn't spray paint.

It was scratch marks. Thousands of them. Names, dates, pleas for help, carved into the rock by desperate hands.

"The Echoes," Amaya whispered.

The tunnel opened into a cavern lit by bioluminescent moss that clung to the ceiling like stars. In the center, a fire burned—not orange, but a cool, steady blue.

Around the fire sat the forgotten.

There were a dozen of them. Some looked like teenagers. Others looked ancient. One man wore the tattered robes of a Curator, but his face was scarred with symbols of silence. A woman with silver braids sat sharpening a knife that looked like it was made of glass.

They looked up as William entered.

"He has the face," the woman with the knife said. She didn't stand. "But does he have the memory?"

"I have a name," William said, stepping into the light. "Jhalia Vynn."

The reaction was instant. The fire flared. The scarred Curator hissed. The woman with the knife stopped sharpening it.

"Do not speak that name here," she said, pointing the glass blade at him. "She is the reason we are here. She is the reason we are nowhere."

"She's rewriting my family," William said, his voice steady. "She's in my house. She's in the ink. And I need to know how to kill her."

The woman stood up. She was tall, her presence filling the cavern. She walked over to William and looked him in the eye.

"You cannot kill a rewrite, boy. You can only overwrite it."

"How?"

"By becoming louder than the lie."

She reached into her pocket and pulled out a small, leather-bound book. It looked like the one his great-grandmother had held in the photo before it turned into a torch.

"This is the Ledger of the Lost," she said. "It contains the names of everyone the Archive decided to forget. We saved them. We wrote them down when no one else would."

She handed it to him.

"The Archive is powerful because it controls the narrative," she said. "But the Echoes? We control the footnotes. And sometimes, the footnotes are where the truth hides."

William opened the book. The pages were filled with names. Thousands of them. And on the very last page, written in fresh ink that still glistened wetly in the blue light, was a new entry.

The Boy Who Will Remember.

"Use it," the woman said. "When the world tries to tell you who you are... read it back to them."

CHAPTER 14

The Breaking Begins

William didn't knock. He walked into Room 207C like he owned the deed.

Professor Morrin stood by the window, watching the sunset. But it wasn't a normal sunset. The clouds were bruised purple, and the light filtering through them looked pixelated, as if the sky were buffering.

"You lied to me," William said, his voice flat. He tossed the Ledger of the Lost onto her desk. It landed with a heavy thud.

Morrin didn't turn. "I taught you," she said. "Lying is omission with intent. I simply waited until you were strong enough to hold the weight."

"You rewrote the prophecy," William said, stepping closer. "The Echoes showed me. You changed the ending."

"I curated it," Morrin corrected, finally turning to face him. Her eyes were tired. The gold iris had dulled to a rusty bronze. "The original prophecy didn't end with a victory, William. It ended with silence. Total, absolute silence. I couldn't let that be the story."

"So you edited it? You gave us false hope?"

"Hope is never false," she said softly. "It is simply a draft we haven't published yet."

"That's semantic garbage, and you know it," William snapped. "You tried to control the narrative, just like the Archive does. And now? Now my mom is forgetting her own name in the laundry room."

Morrin flinched. "Is it that advanced?"

"She didn't recognize me for a full minute. She's fading, Morrin. We all are."

Morrin walked over to the desk and picked up the Ledger. She ran her fingers over the cover, her expression unreadable.

"Every Archive is a battlefield," she whispered. "We tell ourselves we are protecting the past. But really? We are just terrified of the future."

She looked up at him.

"You are right, William. I tried to write a safe ending. But safety is not a story. It's a cage."

She handed the book back to him.

"Go," she said. "Finish it. Not the way I wrote it. The way it happens."

***

That night, the wind didn't blow; it screamed.

William sat on his roof with Jesse and Amaya. The city below them looked normal., cars moving, lights twinkling. But above them, the sky was wrong. The stars were blinking out, one by one, like a string of Christmas lights being unscrewed.

"So," Jesse said, staring upward. "Just to recap. The universe is a giant Word doc, and someone just held down the backspace key."

"Pretty much," William said.

"Cool. Cool, cool, cool." Jesse took a bite of a granola bar. "I'd panic, but honestly? I'm exhausted. If the world ends, at least I don't have to study for trig."

Amaya didn't laugh. She was watching the horizon. "It's not just erasing, Will. It's replacing."

She pointed.

In the distance, the skyline of the city was changing. A skyscraper that had been there yesterday was gone, replaced by a massive, monolithic tower of black stone that pulsed with red light.

"That's not ours," Jesse whispered.

"That's hers," Amaya said. "Jhalia's citadel. She's pasting her reality over ours."

Suddenly, the roof access door creaked open.

Lilith climbed out. She was barefoot, her pajamas fluttering in the unnatural wind. She held her sketchbook against her chest.

"Lil?" William started to get up.

"Sit," she commanded.

She walked over to them and opened the book. The page was glowing.

It was a drawing of the city, split down the middle. One-half was gold and normal. The other half was black and red, consumed by the Rewrite. And in the center, standing on the fault line, was William.

He was holding two scrolls. One was burning. The other was blank.

"They both end the same," Lilith whispered, pointing to the drawing. "But only one remembers."

A sound ripped through the air, like a massive sheet of canvas tearing in half.

William looked up.

Directly above them, the sky split open. A jagged crack of absolute darkness appeared in the purple clouds. And through the crack, a voice boomed—not a voice, but a broadcast, amplified across the entire atmosphere.

UNWRITE.

The streetlights exploded. The cars below stopped moving. The hum of the city died instantly.

"It's here," Amaya said, standing up.

"The Seventh?" Jesse asked, dropping his granola bar.

"No," William said, the ring on his finger burning hot. He stood, clutching the Ledger of the Lost. "The Rewrite."

CHAPTER
15

The Riot of Memory

The world didn't end in a bang. It ended in a buffer.

William stood on the roof, watching the city below stutter. A car driving down Main Street froze, flickered, and then simply wasn't there anymore. The driver was now standing in the middle of the road, looking at his empty hands, confused but not panicked. He just... forgot he was driving.

"It's happening," Amaya whispered. "The Great Edit."

"My mom," William said, turning to the door. "I have to get to my mom."

"Will, wait!" Jesse grabbed his arm. "Look at the school."

William looked.

The school wasn't flickering. It was glowing. A deep, sickly red light pulsed from the auditorium windows, beating in time with the rhythm of the Rewrite.

"They're gathering," Jesse said, his voice trembling. "The assembly. The Principal announced it this morning. Mandatory attendance."

"At night?"

"It started this morning," Jesse said, his eyes wide. "But... did it? Or did we just think it did?" He rubbed his temples. "My head hurts, Will. I can't remember if I ate lunch. I can't remember if I have a third period."

William looked at his friend. The edges of Jesse's silhouette were blurring, like ink bleeding into wet paper.

"We have to stop the broadcast," William said. He looked at Lilith. "Can you stay here? Can you hide?"

Lilith shook her head. She held up her sketchbook. The page showed three figures walking into a red light.

"We go together," she said. "Or we don't go at all."

***

The auditorium was packed. Every student, every teacher, every janitor was there. But it was silent.

Thousands of people sat in the dark velvet seats, staring at the stage. No one was texting. No one was whispering. They were just... receiving.

On the stage, the Principal stood behind a podium that seemed to be growing out of the floorboards, black roots twisting around the wood. His eyes were glazed over, glowing with a faint silver light.

"The past is heavy," the Principal droned. His voice sounded like it was coming from a blown speaker. "Why carry it? Why remember the pain? The failed tests? The broken hearts? Let it go. Let us edit it for you."

The students in the front row nodded in unison. Their eyes glazed over.

"It's a hive mind," Amaya whispered. "He's overwriting their individual memories with a collective narrative."

William gripped the Ledger of the Lost. It felt hot in his hand, vibrating against his palm.

"I have to get to the mic," William said.

"You'll never make it," Jesse said. "Look at the aisles. The Curators."

Standing in the aisles were figures in gray robes. Their faces were smooth, featureless masks. They stood perfectly still, watching the crowd.

"I'll make a distraction," Jesse said.

"Jesse, no—"

"I'm the comic relief, remember?" Jesse offered a weak, terrified smile. "This is literally my only job."

Before William could stop him, Jesse bolted down the center aisle.

"HEY!" Jesse screamed, his voice cracking. "THE PRINCIPAL IS WEARING A TOUPEE! AND THE CAFETERIA PIZZA IS MADE OF CARDBOARD AND SADNESS!"

The silence shattered. Heads turned. The Curators moved, gliding toward Jesse like sharks sensing blood.

"Now!" Amaya shoved William toward the stage.

William sprinted. He vaulted over the orchestra pit, his sneakers slamming onto the stage floor. The Principal turned to him, his silver eyes narrowing.

"Mr. Vale," the Principal distorted. "You are... unauthorized."

"I'm not unauthorized," William said, grabbing the microphone. It squealed with feedback. "I'm the editor."

He turned to the crowd. He looked at the sea of blank faces. He saw his friends. He saw the girl from math class. He saw the bully who stole lunch money. All of them, fading.

He opened the Ledger.

"Don't listen to him!" William shouted into the mic. His voice boomed through the auditorium, shaking the dust from the rafters.

"Listen to you! You are forgetting who you are! You're not just students! You're stories!"

The red light in the room pulsed angrily. The floorboards beneath William groaned, black ink seeping up between the cracks.

"My name is William Vale!" he yelled, reading from the book. "And I remember the meat cubes! I remember the smell of ozone! I remember the names you tried to erase!"

He started reading the names from the Ledger.

"Sarah Jenkins! You broke your arm in third grade on the monkey bars! You cried, but you didn't let go!"

A girl in the third row blinked. The silver light in her eyes faded. She gasped.

"Marcus Hill! You write poetry in the back of your chemistry notebook! You're afraid to show anyone, but it's good!"

A boy in the balcony stood up, shaking his head as if waking from a dream.

"They are trying to make you smooth!" William shouted, the ink now rising around his ankles. "But you are jagged! You are messy! And you are real!"

The Principal lunged at him, his hands turning into claws of black smoke.

But Lilith was there.

She stepped in front of the Principal, small and barefoot. She held up her stone, the one with the open eye.

"Stop," she whispered.

A blast of white light erupted from the stone. It hit the Principal, throwing him back against the curtain.

The red light in the room shattered.

The students gasped, collectively, like a diver breaking the surface. The silence was gone. The auditorium erupted into noise—crying, shouting, remembering.

William dropped the mic. He looked at Amaya. She was smiling, tears streaming down her face.

"You echoed," she mouthed.

William looked down at the Ledger. The ink on the page was settling. The new entry—*The Boy Who Will Remember*—was gone.

In its place, it simply read:

The Author.

CHAPTER 16

The Last Silence Isn't Quiet

The silence that followed wasn't empty. It was full.

It was the sound of a thousand people exhaling at once. It was the rustle of memories returning to their rightful owners—names, dates, petty grudges, secret crushes. The auditorium, which had been a tomb of gray stillness, was suddenly alive with the chaotic, beautiful noise of reality.

William stood on the stage, his chest heaving. The Ledger of the Lost was heavy in his hand, but it no longer burned. It felt cool, solid. Permanent.

Jesse scrambled up the stairs, looking disheveled but undeniably himself.

"Dude," Jesse panted. "I just remembered my middle name. It's Aloysius. My parents really hated me, didn't they?"

William laughed. It was a ragged, exhausted sound, but it was real. "Welcome back, Aloysius."

"Never call me that again." Jesse looked out at the crowd. "So... did we win? Did we beat the final boss?"

"We broke the mute button," Amaya said, joining them. She looked at the Ledger in William's hand. "But the song isn't over."

***

Room 207C was no longer a classroom.

When they returned, the door was gone. The entire wall of the hallway had dissolved, revealing the Archive in its raw form. It wasn't just a room; it was a storm.

Scrolls flew through the air like confused birds. The obsidian table was cracked down the middle. And standing in the center of the chaos, fading like a photograph left in the sun, was Professor Morrin.

"You did it," she said. Her voice sounded distant, as if she were speaking from inside a glass jar.

"We stopped the Rewrite," William said, stepping into the room. The floor felt unstable, shifting like sand.

"You didn't stop it," Morrin corrected gently. "You simply took the pen."

She looked down at her hands. They were becoming translucent. William could see the shelves behind her through her fingers.

"What's happening to you?"

"I am a Curator of the old order, William. My purpose was to protect the silence. The silence is gone. Therefore..." She smiled, a sad, weary expression. "I am being archived."

"Wait," William said, reaching out. "You can't just disappear."

"I'm not disappearing. I'm becoming history. There is a difference."

She looked at him one last time, her mismatched eyes—storm and sun—bright with pride.

"Don't write a safe story, William. Write a true one."

And then, she was gone. Not in a puff of smoke, but like a sentence deleted from a page.

***

"So what now?" Jesse asked.

They were sitting on the steps of the school. The sun was rising, painting the sky in bruises of purple and gold. The world looked normal again—streetlights were fixed, cars were driving—but it felt different. Thinner. Louder.

"Now we wait," Amaya said. She was cleaning her glasses, a habit she'd picked up in the last hour. "The Archive is open. The Echoes are awake. Jhalia's tower is gone, but she isn't."

"She's out there," Lilith said.

She was sitting on the bottom step, drawing in her sketchbook. But she wasn't drawing spirals or glitches anymore. She was drawing a door.

"She's waiting for the ink to dry," Lilith whispered.

William looked at the ring on his finger. It was quiet now. No humming. No heat. Just a piece of old gold that remembered too much.

"Let her wait," William said. He opened the Ledger of the Lost and placed it on his knee. He picked up a pen.

"What are you doing?" Jesse asked.

"Morrin said I'm the Author," William said, looking at the blank page. "I figure I should start writing the sequel."

He wrote one sentence.

The silence is broken.

And somewhere, deep beneath the earth, the Codex hummed in reply.

END OF BOOK 1.

Deep beneath the Archive, something shifted. Not in stone. Not in dust. In the marrow of memory itself.

The Codex did not hum this time. It convulsed.

A ripple tore through its sealed pages, ink lifting from parchment as if trying to flee. The glyphs rearranged violently, burning through languages long buried. Threads of gold snapped and recoiled into black.

Far below the spiraled shelves, beneath the curated histories, beneath the preserved silences, an older chamber trembled.

It had no doors. It had no name. It had been sealed before the First Silence was carved. And now it was awake.

A voice moved through the dark. It did not speak aloud. It pressed itself into the walls, into the ink, into the breath of the Codex.

"He has written."

The words echoed without sound.

A pause followed. Not hesitation. Calculation.

Above, in a small bedroom beneath an ordinary sky, a boy closed his notebook.

Below, the chamber split with a sound like bone under pressure.

One name flickered across the Codex spine.

William Vale.

It did not erase.

It resisted.

The voice deepened.

"Then begin the correction."

The gold threads dimmed. And somewhere in the dark, something began to unwrite.

Series Continues In:

BOOK 2

William and the Library of Unsaid Things

Join the Archive—early art, teacher guides, and a first look at Book Two.

Author's Note

I wrote William and the Seventh Silence for the quiet kids.

The ones who hear too much and say too little. The ones who carry truths in their chest because the world hasn't made space for their voices yet. The ones who feel erased before they even arrive.

This book was born from silence, but not the kind that means peace. The kind that means survival. The kind we inherit. The kind we're told to keep.

William's journey began with a whisper in my mind, a question I couldn't ignore: What if memory could fight back? What if the stories we tried to bury found a way to breathe again?

As a mother, a writer, and a woman shaped by truth and shadow, I wanted to create something that could hold power and softness at the same time. A story where silence is both weapon and wound. A story where Black and brown kids don't have to earn magic, they are the magic.

If you've ever felt like your voice didn't matter, this book is your reminder:

You are the story.

You are the Archive.

And no one can rewrite you.

With love, memory, and fire,

Tigress.

Discussion Guide for Teachers & Book Clubs

About This Guide

This guide is designed to help students explore themes of memory, identity, silence, power, and courage within *William and the Seventh Silence*. The questions and activities can be used for classroom discussion, independent reflection, or small group work.

Discussion Questions

1. What is the Seventh Silence? Why is it considered dangerous?

2. The Archive preserves memory, but it also controls it. Why is control over memory powerful?

3. What does "erasure" represent in the story? Can you think of real-world examples where stories or histories have been erased?

4. William can hear what others cannot. How does this ability shape his identity?

5. When is silence protective? When is silence harmful?

6. The Codex remembers what the Archive tries to forget. Why is it important to preserve forgotten stories?

7. What does it mean to be an "Author" in the story? How does writing become power?

8. How do friendship and loyalty influence William's choices?

9. If you were a Keeper, what truth would you protect?

10. What message does the novel send about voice and identity?

Classroom & Creative Activities

Activity 1: Write Your Own "Silence"

Ask students to imagine a "Silence" in their own world—something important that is often ignored or unspoken.
Write a short paragraph explaining:

1. What the Silence represents

2. Why it exists

3. What might happen if it were broken

Activity 2: Rewrite a Forgotten Story

Students choose a historical event, family story, or cultural tradition that is often overlooked.
Write a short "Codex Entry" preserving that memory.

Activity 3: Design Your Own Codex Page

Students create a visual Codex entry including:

1. A symbol

2. A short prophecy or warning

3. A memory that must be protected

Extension Questions for Older Students (Grades 7-8)

1. How does the novel explore institutional control?

2. Is truth always safe? Why or why not?

3. Can memory itself be weaponized?